MEN UNDER MY SHEETS

UNAPOLOGETICALLY

J.J

Made with ❤ on the Notion Press Platform
www.notionpress.com

To every man who passed by me,

Thank you for the content.....

Unapologetically

J.J......

Contents

CHAPTER I

Intimate Reflections

In certain moments, the vast expanse of my world seems to shrink into a precarious thread of uncertainty, a fragile line where the boundaries between lust and love become hazy. It's a delicate balance that, especially when entwined with men beneath the sheets, often blurs .

Wrapped in layers of intimacy, my encounters become a journey into the depths of desire. As the skin embraces me, it's an alluring invite to explore what is beneath the embrace.As the world beyond dissolves, men reveal concealed aspects of themselves within a hidden realm, a space shielded from the mundane. Here, desires and passions weave through the intricacies of reality, grappling with fears, insecurities, and the essence of life itself. The once clear line between elements blurs, transforming what initially appeared as a genuine allure into a profound warmth resembling love.

Venturing beneath the surface of intimacy prompts a ponderous question:

Is the sensation akin to love , or is it merely a play of perception?

Am I simply being vulnerable, or is it simply a shared human experience to feel this way?

Why does a one-night stand cast an emotional cocoon that lingers until the morning departure?

Going beyond the mere physical, this journey dives into the intricate world of emotions and human bonds. It raises questions about the genuine nature of the feelings that surface during those intimate moments beneath the sheets

1

. I often try to delve into the truth in these emotions woven into the fabric of our shared experiences, the complexities of emotions and human connections. The very end , I end up questioning the authenticity of feelings that arise in the intimate moments shared beneath the sheets.

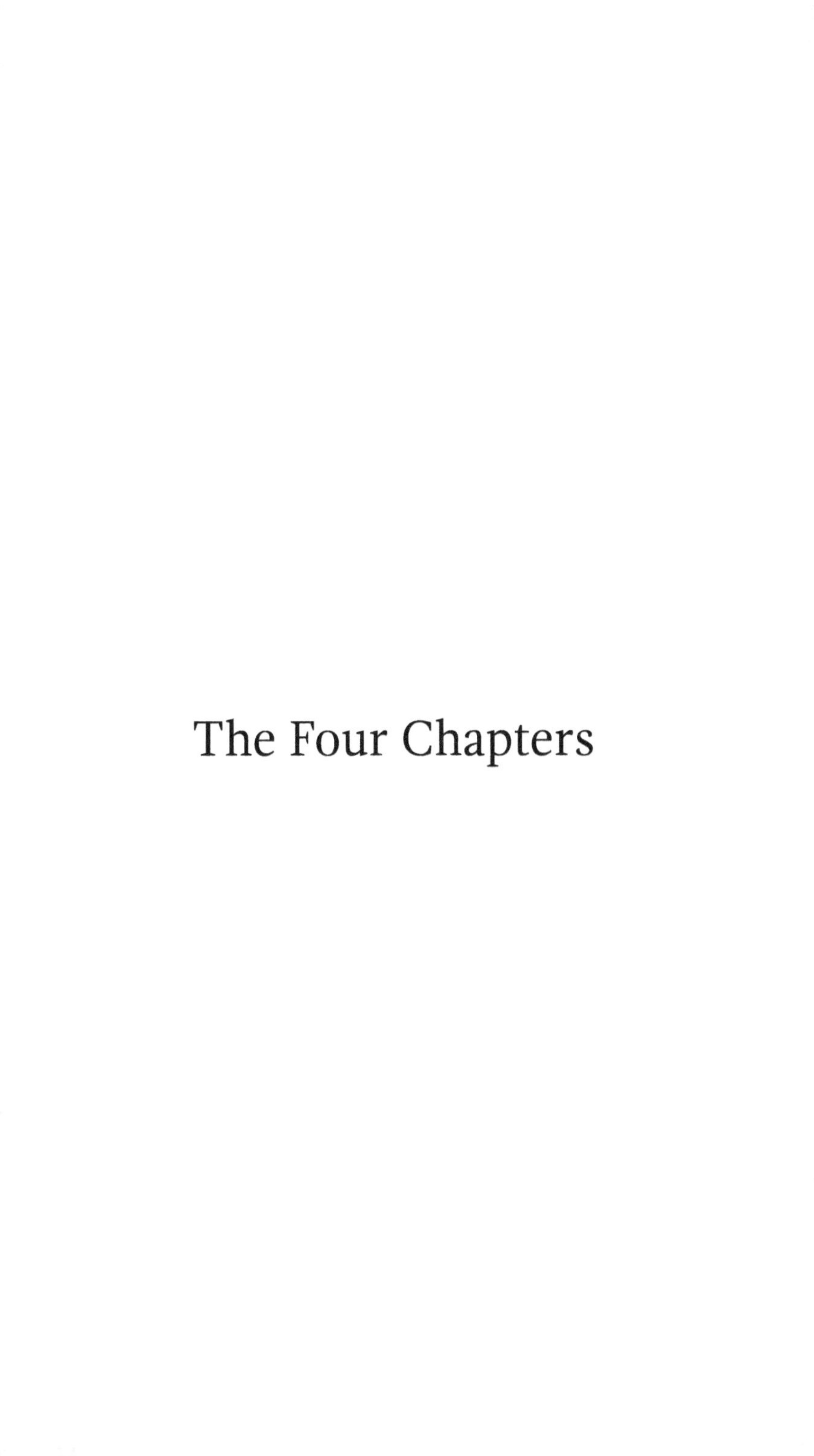

The Four Chapters

CHAPTER II

The Powerful Whisperer

"Are you enjoying it?", he murmured as we both stood in front of the mirror, our naked bodies reflected back at us.

Balancing on my toes, I relished the changing hues on my face while he enveloped me from behind, delving into me with increasing intensity.

I fed him like a mother, while his skillful fingers explored my wet desires, parting my legs to create a path for him to delve into.

He was both the masterpiece and the artist, relentless even as my cries persisted as my breathlessness failed to satiate him.

Every nerve in my body tingled with ecstasy as we surrendered to the rhythm of our shared pleasure. His dominant presence on top of me commanded our intimate moments, each forceful stroke accompanied by his gaze that locked onto mine.

"Take this," he declared, delivering powerful sensations that elicited my loudest moans. His authoritative eyes met mine, and in the aftermath, we embraced, breathless and heartbeats racing.

Running my fingers through his hair, I planted a tender kiss on his forehead. Briefly, he withdrew for a few seconds, but then held me closer, vulnerable and nestled against my chest, much like a contented baby.

Amidst the tender embraces, his vulnerability surfaced, and the once formidable figure now cradled against my chest, shedding tears like a tender soul. Nestled in my embrace, seeking solace, our paths crossed for the first and final time.

Without prying into the reasons behind his tears, I held him close with a motherly embrace. Unspoken queries lingered—was it familial pain, a departed love? I chose not to delve into the details. A serene silence enveloped us. However, the intensity of his gaze never returned, leaving an unspoken barrier between us.

Was it the fear of unraveling emotions that kept you from meeting my eyes again?

CHAPTER III

A Virgin To Keep

A virgin is a trophy.

I positioned myself squarely before him, drawing down the zipper of my dress until it surrendered entirely to my touch.

"Happy Birthday" , I said .

Once amidst the familiarity of his home where I often visited to see his mother, he revealed the depths of his longing in hushed tones. In that instant, a transformation swept over him, casting aside the shades of his youth to embody the essence of manhood. It was then that I came to the realization that I had mistaken his lingering gazes, once dismissed as innocent curiosity, for a more lustful desire. His kiss was tender as his hands caressed me, his whispered words painting a vivid picture of possession. "I want a ride with you," he declared.

He adorned my lips with the remnants of his birthday cake before embracing me with hunger. The chocolate ganache from his mouth cascaded over my nakedness, melding with his touch and taste. With him bound to the bed, now adorned with cream and marked by the traces of our passion,I felt the pressure of his eager hands upon my flesh.His gaze fixated, yearned for nothing but the sweetness of the moment. As I mounted on his face, he eagerly indulged, his tongue delving deep in search of more chocolatey bliss. In our frenzy, I unleashed my wildness, spurred on by his fervor, going back and forth and letting his tongue do a chocolate swirl.

"I love you ," he murmured, as he savored his first shots. There was an intensity to him.In between our twists and turns, he explored my deepest trenches. He gripped my hair firmly, taking me beyond the confines of the world I knew. An ardent lover he is.

I straddled him, letting my hair free. His hands roamed behind my hair, exploring my curves eagerly. With each move, his touch grew more urgent and strong. Locking eyes with him,I savored the sensation of his fingers in my mouth, feeling his pleasure-filled gasp as I was inside him. With my hands raised above my head, I let out soft moans, gently tugging at my hair, revealing his hands on my breasts. As I rode him up and down, making the world around us cease to exist, he gasped again "I love you ," while I danced him to the peaks before marking his coming out as a man."

"But, I am no keeper , my love", I muttered to myself , kissing the sleepy birthday boy goodbye forever.

CHAPTER IV

The Opaque Man

Beneath the layers of sheets, the world is very opaque.

As a mistress, I realized I was not alone in the role. I chuckled at my own folly, recognizing the depth of the emotional pain I had allowed myself to endure.

My mind played back to a few months prior when he, on the brink of departing for his home, enveloped me with a sense of security. Rocking gently atop me, he whispered in my ears, "I promise I won't go to anyone else." That utterance held the weight of a solemn commitment, a unique weight, etched into the very fabric of shared passion.

In the realm of love, a woman's devotion knows no bounds.

Questions lingered.....

Why make promises?

Why weave words into a fabric of belief?

It appeared that opacity was a characteristic more frequently associated with men. Alternatively, could it be that I was simply too transparent, making myself vulnerable ?

Then comes moments when he faces a decision, seeking labels for me- a mistress, a third party, or a side squeeze- an unmistakable signal that it's time for me to part ways.

When the choice is made, the weight of the assured words revealed the fragility of the emotions accompanied

I refrain from casting my gaze back upon such men, for their presence weighs heavily. The commitments of 'love' and 'togetherness' loom large over the path traveled. Yet, it encourages reflecting on oneself and mastering the skill of letting go.

Men are not trees indeed.

CHAPTER V

The Untouchable

In the quiet intimacy of the room, I couldn't help but ask him playfully, "Are you going to draw my portrait ?" His laughter filled the space as he adjusted his chair closer to my bedside. "I just like watching you like this," he replied softly. For the next ten minutes, silence enveloped us with him doing nothing but gazing at my naked body.

I adore my nakedness. I find a certain allure in my own sensuality that turns me on. Self pleasure is a luxury that turns on men. As my hand trailed down my stomach, seeking the warmth between my thighs, the naked soul before me rose from his chair, drawn to my desires like a moth to flame. I parted my knees and stroked my wet lips .His gaze delved into the depths of my arousal.Without laying a finger on me, he breathed in the essence of my desires, inhaling deeply as if savoring the scent of my longing. A sense of untouchability lingered within him.

" Finger yourself ", he commanded

Half lost in ecstasy, I obeyed, fingers delving into my slick folds while he recorded the symphony of my moans in his phone. With a primal hunger, he knelt before me, his tongue tracing patterns of pleasure along my trembling flesh.His tongue glided along the length to the tip, lapping up my essence before parting my lips with a skillful touch. He devoured me eagerly, like a beaver gnawing at its prize, while I fought to maintain my composure amidst waves of pleasure. My screams echoed in the room as he ensured I reached heights of ecstasy I had never experienced before. Nothing touched me but his tongue, and all he desired was the space between my thighs, as if he craved it for eternity.

Orgasm after orgasm washed over me, yet still, I yearned for more, Rising to his feet, he beckoned me to sit on his face, his own desire palpable beneath me. As I lowered myself onto him, he initiated a rhythmic motion moving my parted legs with precision, almost like a well-oiled machine. Occasionally, he'd implore me to let him drink from me allowing him to draw out the very essence of my being. Never before had I been so overcome with arousal, and yet here I was, left sore for days by a man who seemed untouchable yet possessed the power to leave me utterly undone.

"You taste like pumpkin and egg soup," he murmured as I dressed, a playful comment that brought a smile to my lips.

"Wait, I'm not finished," he declared, playing the recording before shutting his eyes and indulging in his own pleasure as my cries echoed throughout the room once more.

Is it me or you, the untouchable in this story ??

CHAPTER VI

The Awakening

In the stillness of dawn, the soft light filtered through the curtains, casting gentle shadows on the bed. My thoughts drifted to the men who had crossed my path, each leaving an indelible mark on my soul. The blurred line between lust and love, between physical pleasure and emotional connection, had become a constant in my life. But now, I am yearning for clarity.

Epilogues

CHAPTER VII

The Powerful Whisperer

His memories remain vivid.

In the days that followed, I found myself reflecting on the complexity of emotions we had shared. His dominance, the way he commanded our moments together, was balanced by an unexpected tenderness that surfaced in the quiet aftermath. It was in those silent, tear-filled embraces that I saw a part of him few others ever would—a raw, unguarded soul seeking solace in my arms.

Despite the intensity of our connection, we never met again. The barrier that rose between us, built on unspoken fears and unresolved emotions, was insurmountable. Perhaps he feared the depth of what he felt, the possibility of unravelling emotions he had long kept at bay. Or maybe it was I who feared that delving too deep into his pain would expose my own hidden wounds.

In the time since, I have come to realize that our encounter was a powerful reminder of the delicate balance between strength and vulnerability. It taught me that even the most formidable of us can harbor deep-seated pain, and that true intimacy lies in the willingness to share those hidden parts of ourselves.

I often wonder where he is now, whether he has found the peace he sought in my embrace. I hope he has come to terms with whatever haunted him that night. As for me, I have embraced the lessons learned from our brief, intense connection. I have learned to value the moments of genuine connection, however fleeting, and to cherish the vulnerability that comes with true intimacy.

Our paths may never cross again, but the powerful whispers of that night will forever echo in my mind. They serve as a testament to the beauty and complexity of human connection, reminding me that within the depths of our desires lies the potential for profound emotional resonance.

And so, I move forward, carrying with me the memory of his touch, his tears, and the unspoken bond we shared.

Indeed for one night, we were able to break down the walls that separated us and touch each other's souls .

CHAPTER VIII

A Virgin To Keep

A year had passed since the newfound manhood. The memory of his birthday lingered in the recesses of my mind, a vivid tableau of passion and discovery.

On the eve of his next birthday, a message appeared on my phone: "Hey, it's me. I can't stop thinking about last year. Can we meet again?" His words were filled with longing, an echo of the intensity we had shared. For a moment, I was tempted, drawn by the memory of his eager touch and whispered declarations of love.

There exists within many women a powerful inclination to enslave men, to bind them with the chains of desire and emotional dependence. It is a force that can be both intoxicating and dangerous. . I had felt this pull with him in our encounter. I had glimpsed the potential to dominate, to become the center of his world, and it had frightened me.

Our night together had been transformative for him, a passage from boyhood to manhood. I had seen the way his eyes lingered on me, the way his hands trembled with both awe and need. He had looked at me as though I were his entire universe. But with that adoration came a responsibility I was not prepared to bear. I did not want to bind him to me with invisible chains, to become a figure he could never fully escape.

"Happy birthday.. Our night was special, but it was a one-time thing. You deserve to find someone who can be there for you in every way. Take care."

As I hit send, a sense of melancholy washed over me. The decision was the right one, but it did not come without its pangs of sorrow. I had given him a piece of myself, and in doing so, I had also taken a piece of him.

In my refusal, lies a wisdom which I hope he understands. Love, after all, is not just about possession or repetition. It is about growth and self-discovery. By letting him go, I was giving him the space to find a deeper, more enduring love—one that would stand the test of time.

Our encounter had been deep, but it was never meant to be repeated.

CHAPTER IX

The Opaque Man

The opaque man remains a shadow in my past, a ghost that neither haunts nor departs. He never reached back, and I never extended my hand. Our silence, an unspoken pact, sealed the fissures of a once-shared world.

I wear a strong face, a mask of resilience that others admire. In the eyes of the world, I have moved on and embraced new beginnings. Yet, in the quiet solitude of my thoughts, I often wonder. Did I merely fill the gaps in his life, a temporary solace in his quest for completeness?

There are moments when his words echo in the corners of my mind, "I promise." They are no longer a source of pain but a reminder of my own vulnerability and the depth of my capacity to love. I reflect on the opacity that once surrounded him and the transparency I offered so willingly.

This reflection is not tinged with bitterness but with a quiet understanding. I recognize the lessons learned and the strength gained from the experience. The path of letting go is not linear, and sometimes, it feels like I am standing still. But in truth, I am not the same person who once lay beneath those layers of sheets, enveloped in a false sense of security.

I have grown, evolved, and found solace in my own company. The opaque man may never know the journey I have taken, nor the strength it has required. But in the end, it is my journey, my story, and I hold the pen.

In the realm of love, I have discovered that devotion is not just to another, but to oneself. Men are not trees, rooted and immovable. And neither am I.

I am a river, flowing forward, carrying the essence of my experiences while continually moving towards the horizon.

CHAPTER X

The Untouchable

A week later, I received a message from him. "Can we meet again?" it read. His words lingered on the screen, a siren's call to return to the intoxicating world we had created together. I paused, contemplating my response. Was I ready to step into that realm of untouchability once more, or was it time to seek connections that offered both passion and emotional resonance?

As I pondered, I realized that the answer lay not in him, but in me. Our encounter had been a dance of untamed desire, a symphony of pleasure that left me breathless and sore for days. Yet, amidst the ecstasy, there was a sense of distance, an impenetrable barrier that neither of us had truly breached. He was untouchable in his own way, driven by a primal hunger that sought only the physical, leaving the emotional untouched and unexplored.

But was it not me who had erected those barriers first? In my pursuit of self-indulgence and control, had I not kept my heart guarded, allowing only the carnal to dominate our interactions? The power to touch or remain untouched was mine, a choice I had made in the heat of passion and now faced once more.

With a smile, I replied, "Let's see where the journey takes us." It was an invitation, not just to him, but to myself. An invitation to explore the depths of my own desires and boundaries, to understand what I truly sought from these encounters. Would I remain the untouchable, savoring the fleeting pleasures of the flesh, or would I open my heart to the possibility of something more?

As I sent the message, a sense of calm washed over me. The journey ahead was uncertain, filled with the promise of both pleasure and potential pain. Yet, it was a path I was willing to tread, guided by the knowledge that the power to shape my experiences lay within me. Whether I chose to touch or remain untouched, to seek the ephemeral or the enduring, the decision was mine alone.

In the quiet aftermath of our encounter, I had discovered a profound truth. The essence of intimacy lies not just in the physical connection, but in the willingness to be vulnerable, to allow oneself to be touched in ways that go beyond the flesh. As I awaited his response, I felt a sense of anticipation, not just for the pleasure that awaited, but for the journey of self-discovery that lay ahead.

Whatever the future held, I was ready to embrace it, one intimate moment at a time.

Beyond The Sheets

As I sit here, reflecting on the intricate tapestry of my encounters, I come to a profound realization: it's not about the men, it's about me. Each story, each intimate moment shared beneath the sheets, has been a journey of self-discovery, a quest to understand the depths of my desires, my vulnerabilities, and my capacity for love.

In the powerful whispers of passion, the untouchable allure of fleeting desire, and the bittersweet farewell of missed connections, I have found echoes of my own longing, my own yearning for connection and understanding. It is in these moments that I have come to understand the complexities of human emotion, the delicate balance between strength and vulnerability, between lust and love.

From each encounter, I have chosen to extract valuable lessons, to learn from the experiences that have shaped me, and to let go of the burdens that no longer serve me. I have learned that true intimacy lies not in the physical act itself, but in the willingness to be open, to be vulnerable, to allow oneself to be touched in ways that go beyond the surface. It is in the moments of shared passion, the whispered confessions of desire, and the silent embraces of solace that I have found the true essence of connection.

But I have also learned to discern between fleeting pleasure and lasting fulfillment, between the allure of physical attraction and the depth of emotional resonance. I have learned to listen to my own intuition, to trust in my own judgment, and to honor my own needs and desires above all else.

And so, as I close these chapters of my life, I realize that I am no longer defined by the men who have crossed my path, but by the strength and resilience I have discovered within myself.

I am a woman who knows what she wants, who is unafraid to explore the depths of her desires, and who understands that true intimacy begins with self-discovery. I am not defined by the men I have loved or lost, but by the journey of self-exploration that has led me to this moment.

As I step forward into the unknown, I do so with a renewed sense of purpose and self-assurance. I am no longer seeking validation or fulfillment from others, but from within myself. I am a woman who knows her worth, who embraces her desires, and who is unafraid to chart her own course.

And so, as I bid farewell to these four men beneath the sheets, I do so with a sense of gratitude for the role they have played in my journey. They have been mirrors reflecting back the depths of my desires, the complexities of my emotions, and the strength of my spirit.

But now, as I stand on the thresholds of new chapters, I do so with a sense of clarity and self-assurance. I am no longer searching for love or validation from others, but from within myself. I am a woman who knows her worth, who embraces her desires, and who is unafraid to chart her own course.

In the end, it is not about the men, it is about me. And as I am ready to embark on the next chapters of my life, I do so with a sense of excitement and anticipation for the adventures that lie ahead.

For I am a woman who is unafraid to explore the depths of her desires, to embrace her vulnerabilities, and to love herself fiercely and unapologetically.